1

Life to the MAX

Maxims for a Great Life
by a Dog named Max

as told to my mom, Robin Reynolds

Always remember to live
"Life to the MAX!"

nice CREATIVE

3

ISBN: 978-0-9795294-0-5

Designed by  nice
CREATIVE®

10 9 8 7 6 5 4 3 2

Published by NICE Creative
a division of Robin Reynolds Creative, Inc.
4645 South Lakeshore Drive
Suite 16
Tempe, AZ 85282
www.nicecreative.com

4

This book is for:

_____

With doggone good wishes from:

_____

Dedication

This book is for **Andrew**.
May you always be grateful for the lessons
you learn and for those who teach you.
I love you.

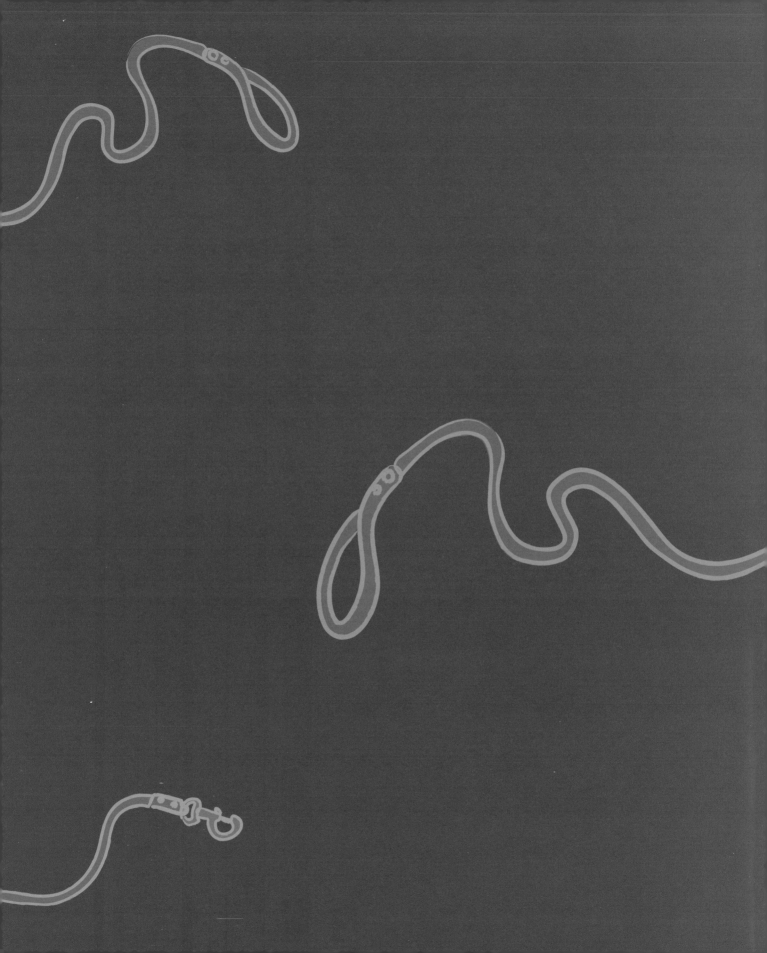

Life to the MAX

Maxims for a Great Life
by a Dog named Max

Some people say

we are all sent to this earth to learn certain lessons and our teachers can come in some surprising forms. The smallest child. The most distant relative. Or even a rowdy, scraggly-haired quadruped like me. Of course, I wasn't always scraggly-haired. In fact, I was downright **haaand-some,** as you can see.

Yup, this is me, Max. For those of you who don't know, I'm a part of a special breed fondly referred to as Airedale "Terrors." I think that means we have **personality** and **spirit,** but I've also heard us described as determined, willful or even stubborn. (I think that's a little harsh.) As a group though, we're really pretty smart, playful and (did I mention?) **haaand-some!**

Of course, I'm a little unusual even for my breed. You see, all my life I've had black ears. Most Airedales start out with black ears and the color fades as they grow up. But mine didn't. On top of that, my legs and face are the color of champagne. (I know the color is really called "grizzle," but doesn't "champagne" sound better?) My fur is coarse and wiry, but when I'm washed and brushed, it's as soft as big tufts of cotton. It puffs out my legs and chest, masking my Greyhound-like thinness underneath. Even those who know my breed realize I'm a special dude—not just for the way I look, but more for the lessons I taught my friends and family. This is my story about those lessons and how I lived life to the **MAX!**

11

As I write this, I've lived twelve and a half great years. Well, maybe twelve great years. You see, before I met my true family, I lived with another family, which wasn't so great.

I suppose they were excited when they first brought me home. I'm sure I was a cute puppy. But maybe I grew bigger than they thought I would. Maybe I was too rambunctious or I got too dirty. All I know is that when I was seven months old, I was put in a car and taken to a place called the Humane Society.

The people I met there were very nice. They patted my head and scratched my ears. They checked to make sure I was healthy and they all told me I was **haaand-some**.

I was having a good time greeting everyone—until they led me into a large room that was lined with kennels filled with other dogs who were barking and crying. As they coaxed me into the kennel and shut the door, I began to feel scared and started to pace. What's going to happen to me? Where did everyone go? When are my owners coming back? I began to howl along with the other dogs, when I heard a couple of the workers coming toward my kennel.

"We need a dog to feature on 'Pet of the Week,' Ed, and I know the perfect one. He just came in."

A man with a cheerful face and kind eyes peered into my kennel and smiled. "You're gonna be a TV dog," he assured me as he opened the door. "We just have to clean you up a little."

Wow! A TV dog! I didn't know what that meant, but I figured it must be something good. This was going to be a **great day** after all! (Better than being locked in a cage, anyway.)

Maxim #1:

When **bad things happen**,
worrying won't change anything.

Trust you'll get through it.

When they first hoisted me into a truck, I was excited to be going for a ride. But then I was taken to a groomer where I was totally immersed in something called tick dip (which is really something I don't care to repeat). Then I was scrubbed and brushed until my fur hurt (which was quite an ordeal considering how dirty and matted it was). By the time, I was brought back to the Humane Society, I felt like a pinball. I leapt off the truck as if a firecracker was tied to my tail and landed right at the feet of my mom and dad (although at the time, I didn't know they were going to be my parents.)

My mom and dad had been working with the Airedale Rescue Association to find a friend for the Airedale they already had. The rescue people had told them I was at the Humane Society. My dad got mixed up about where to go, so my mom and dad had gone to the dog pound first and then raced over to the Humane Society. They arrived just five minutes before closing time and just as the workers were bringing me back from the groomer. I must have been quite a sight as I hurdled off that truck—all wiggly and wild. My dad tried to pet me, but I just danced around.

My dad stood up, "I dunno maybe we should bring Bernie over and see how they get along."

But Mom looked deep into my eyes. "No, let's just take him home."

Wow! This is a great day!

Because my mom and dad went to the wrong place, we all arrived at the Humane Society at just the right time to meet each other. I don't think there are any accidents. People come into your life for a reason.

Maxim #2:

Trust that you'll meet
just the **right people** at
just the **right time**.

After my mom and dad finished all the paperwork, the man behind the counter scratched me under my chin. "Well fella, I'm sure glad you found a family, but we're sure sorry we're not gonna have such a handsome guy for our TV dog." I wagged my tail to show my appreciation.

Then my parents took me out to my new car and I leapt happily into the back seat. As we drove home, my mom read from some of the papers. "It says here his name is "Scoochies," She turned to me and called, "Hey, Scoochies. Scoochies!"

I looked out the window.

Mom turned back to Dad "If he was so well taken care of, why was he so dirty and why doesn't he know his name?" She stretched out her hand to pat my head, "This poor dog has been neglected, if not abused."

Of course, there were things I couldn't tell my parents about life before, but they just seemed to know.

Then my mom turned to me and called, "Hey King!"

Again, I gazed out the window.

"Here, Duke!"

I put my head down and sighed.

She looked at me for several moments. I saw her face light up.
"Hey, Max!"

A smile consumed my whole body. I stood up and smiled so wide I exposed my overbite and wagged my whole back half.

"Look at how he's smiling!" my dad laughed.
"This dog's name is **Max.**"

16

Maxim #3:

Treasure the people
who can **see** you
for who you **really** are.

When we arrived home, my mom went in the front door and my dad brought me through a gate into the backyard.

"Where are we going, Dad? Where's Mom? Oooh, this is a nice yard. Can I pee on this tree? Oh look, there's Mom!! Hey, who's with Mom? She looks a lot like me. Can I go see? CanIcanIcanI? (PULLLL-INNG, PULLLL-INNG!) Sniff, sniff. Hi, hi, who are you? Smiling, wagging all over. You're Bernie? I'm Max. Hey watch where you're sniffing, Bernie, you're getting kind of personal. You want to run, Bernie? Okay, leash is off! Let's gooooooo...!"

The next thing I knew, we were running up and down the backyard, having the best time. A new family, a new friend! This is a great day!

Maxim #4:

Even after the
worst experiences,
the **best** things
can happen.

Bernie and I went on to be the best of pals, though she made sure I knew she was queen. Whenever I did something she didn't like, she'd let me know by biting my head. Not hard, just enough to let me know who was boss. Of course, she did blame me for stuff I had nothing to do with—like when my mom used the blender and Bernie didn't like the noise, she'd bite my head. The doorbell would ring, she'd bite my head. She wanted to be petted first when Mom and Dad came home, **she'd bite my head.**

Mostly, we got along really well. My favorite was when she would hold me down and lick my ears until I let out a big, loud sigh of contentment. **Aaaaah-mmmmm!**

I guess I sighed a lot. At bedtime, I would circle around… and around…. and around……. on my bed. Sometimes after about 15 minutes, my mom and dad would yell, "Max, lie down!" They didn't understand finding the perfect spot takes time. But when I did lay down, every muscle would relax and I would let out a big groan and sigh of contentment. **Aaaaah-mmmmm!**

Dad told Mom that maybe I had the right idea. After that, when Dad got into bed, he'd let out a great big, groaning sigh. **Aaaaah-mmmmm!**

When Dad did it though, Mom sometimes hit him with a pillow.

Maxim #5:

To completely **relax**,
let out a great big,
      groaning sigh.
Aaaaah-mmmmm!

When I came to live with Mom, Dad and Bernie, I was so lucky to be introduced to a lot of special people. Dr. Wight, Dr. Claus and the staff at the animal clinic always cared for me like I was family.

Dr. Wight, my primary vet, had big, expressive eyes that danced when she talked and a smile that animated her whole face. Her voice surged with her obvious passion and love of animals. Many times, she would bury her head in the nape of my neck and give me kisses. I think it's possible she was an Airedale in another life!

Dr. Claus had a calming effect on all of us. Strong and gentle, she was the surgeon who helped me through both the routine and unexpected procedures I faced during my life.

The whole staff made the clinic a welcome place to go. Bernie was a little scared to go there, but I was always happy and glad to see everyone.

"Hello, Ladies! The Max-erator is in the house!"

Everyone just lit up when they saw me. "Max, how's our happy boy?" Back half wagging, teeth bared, I gave them my best smile. I sometimes managed to scare a few landscapers, delivery guys and cleaning ladies with that goofy grin. But these guys were cool. "Max, you are always smiling!"

Yeah, they really seemed to appreciate me for the stud I was—even if they were responsible for fixing me. Oh yeah, **I'm the dawg!**

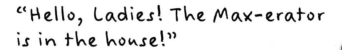

Maxim #6:

Great vets are more
than just **doctors**,
they're **family**.

Because of my experience with the tick dip and everything, I was a little skittish about going to a groomer again. But I could tell Shelly, my new groomer, really enjoyed grooming me. She would talk to me so tenderly as she washed me. Then she would painstakingly clip, trim and brush me until I looked like a **show dog**. Only once did she make the mistake of tying bows into my furnishings. But Bernie saved me from embarrassment. She chewed them off as soon as I got home. After that, Shelly always adorned me more appropriately with a jaunty little **bandana** around my neck.

Maxim #7:

A good groomer
is vital to your
self-esteem.

Mom and Dad took Bernie and me just about everywhere. They took us on hikes in the desert and trips in the car. They took us to the park and let us run off-leash—until I got distracted by a dog in a yard far away. Then I'd run off with my Dad chasing me and calling my name to no avail. They took us

up north and let us romp in the snow. They took us to see their friends, like Bob, who used to jump around with us until Bernie got so excited she'd pee on the floor.

We loved it when the massage therapist would come to visit (Mom and Dad, not us.) My parents would make us sit with our tails impatiently beating the carpet while she set up her massage table. Then after several agonizing minutes she would call us. We would run like madmen into the bedroom, jumping on her and each other until we got our ears massaged. **"Ohhhh honey,** you got the spot. Right there. Oh yes! Now my leg is thumping! Bernie, it is not your turn! **Quit biting my head!"**

Almost every Sunday, Dad would also take us running with one of his friends. We always knew when it was Sunday because Dad would lay out his running stuff the night before. Though we would be up before Dad could even lace up his shoes, Bernie would actually sleep by the door just to make sure we wouldn't be left behind. Bernie and I thought it was kind of funny that Dad

and his friend called it "running" because we were just walking fast. Still, it was great to get out in the cool morning air and strut our stuff on the running path—then back home for a well-deserved nap. This is the **life!**

Maxim #8:

Get the most out of **life**
by doing things
you **enjoy!**

Then there were our birthday parties. Mom and Dad didn't know exactly when my birthday was. The Humane Society paperwork had indicated that I was born in February, so they decided to celebrate my birthday on Valentine's Day.

Mom would put birthday hats on us and give us dog ice cream. Bernie and I didn't like the hat part very much, but we humored my parents because we knew they really needed kids. Still, no kids came to our family.

Then one night, I heard my mom talking to my dad about adoption, but Dad was unsure.

"I dunno," he said, "I'm just not sure if I could bond."

Mom took my dad's hand. "I know it isn't exactly the same thing, but look at Max. We didn't own him first, but look how much we love him and how bonded he is to us."

I looked up at my dad and wagged my tail for emphasis. My dad slowly ran his hand over my head and down my back. Then as he hugged my neck, I felt his heart open in a way I'd never felt before. I knew at that moment I had made a difference in my dad's life just by being me.

What a great day!

Maxim #9:

Help someone else
by sharing the
gift of you.

It wasn't too long after that Andrew came to make our family complete. I liked to sniff him, but he kind of spooked me. He was so little and inquisitive and **annoying**.

So I left Bernie to play with him most of the time, as she was much more patient than me. She loved to let Andrew crawl all over her and she'd just lick him when she'd had enough.

But that stuff made me jittery. Still, we had some of the best times together—chasing bubbles, running around the backyard and just playing together. By the time Andrew was older, we were best pals!

Maxim #10:

A family
is made by love,
not necessarily DNA.

After Andrew arrived, Mom and Dad decided to find a new home with a larger yard that had more room for Andrew and us to play. I sometimes wonder exactly when they started thinking about a new house. Maybe it all started innocently enough that one afternoon when, as usual, Bernie and I were tearing around the backyard.

"Chase me, chase me, Bernie! Ha ha, can't catch me! Ouch, Bernie! Quit biting my head! Oh watch out, Bernie! The ledge around the pool is narrow. Bernie, you're pushing me! ARGH!" (SPLASH!)

I struggled to the edge of the pool and tried to pull myself up on the deck, but my thick, wet fur pulled me under. Glub! Glub! Bernie began to jump up and down and bark furiously. Then all of sudden, I saw this figure in a long white robe standing above me. I was swimming vertically and gasping for air. HELP! GLUB, GLUB!! As I went under the water again, the figure reached down, grabbed me by the collar and pulled me out of the water.

After I was out and shook, Bernie came right over and bit my head. Then I looked for this angel who had saved me and realized it was Mom in a bathrobe. She was all wet after I had shaken water all over her, but she never looked better to me. Mom and Dad had been planning to put up a pool fence before Andrew arrived anyway, but now they accelerated the schedule. I didn't mind that the pool fence made our already small backyard even smaller because it also made it safer.

Maxim #11:

People who **really love you**
will **be there** when
you need them **most.**

So we moved to our new house. Here the yard was big and open with lots of area to play. Bernie and I immediately discovered that there were dogs that lived on either side of us. Bernie liked to bark at the dog on one side of the house and at the same time, I liked to bark at the dog on the other side. **Cool, it was like stereo!** But I didn't just like to bark. I liked to jump up four or five feet in the air to try to see him. My mom would sometimes say, "Max, cut that out you're going to give yourself a bad back." Of course, I didn't listen.

Maxim #12:

Parents get **smarter**
as you get **older**.

Well, time went happily by like this for years. Then one day, after I was at the groomer, Shelly called my parents to say she had found a growth on my foot. Later, after Dr. Wight examined me and ran some tests on the growth, I heard her tell my parents it was a melanoma and she needed to remove my toe. My parents were worried about how I would react after the surgery. But I trotted right out. **"That's over. No big deal,"** I thought. But Dr. Wight was very thorough. She told my parents she wanted me to see a specialist.

So a few days later, we got in the car and drove to another vet's hospital. While I was busy sniffing around, I heard the oncologist tell my parents that the melanoma could easily spread even though the toe had been removed. It was possible I could beat the cancer with chemotherapy, but at best she gave me two years.

All of a sudden I saw that Mom was choking back tears. I came over and laid my head in her lap. "Don't cry, Mom. It'll be okay."

"Will he be nauseous and lose his fur?" she asked the oncologist as she caressed my head. The vet shook her head. "No, it's not the same for animals as people. You probably won't see a difference."

Mom and Dad exchanged looks. "We have to give him a chance," Dad said as he squeezed Mom's hand. She nodded.

After that, I went through a series of chemotherapy treatments. Many of the dogs who were undergoing the same thing at the same time didn't seem too happy and sometimes resisted going with the technician. But not me. I just smiled and pranced right along, happy to greet the world each day. But even after the chemo was over, it didn't completely end there, because there were more growths and more toes removed. I also became a little hard of hearing and developed a heart arrhythmia. Still, if it hurt, I never complained because I knew my parents had given me another chance.

Every day just had to be a **great day!**

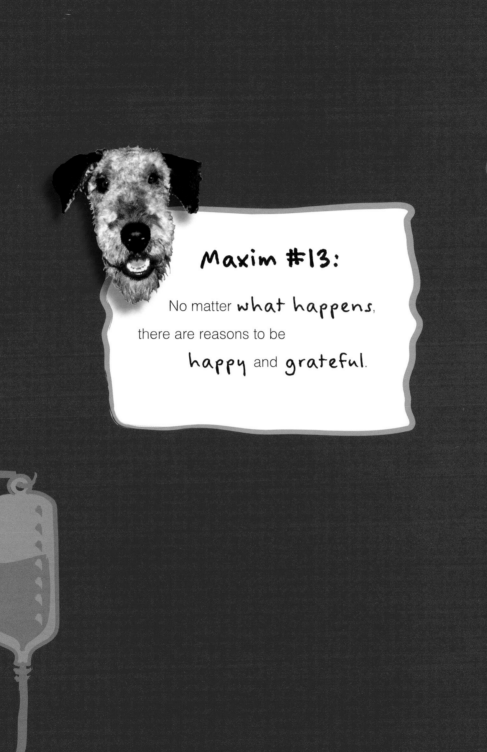

Maxim #13:

No matter **what happens,**
there are reasons to be

happy and **grateful.**

One Sunday when I woke up, I wasn't the one that was hurting. Bernie was panting hard and when Dad touched her stomach, she yelped. I heard Dad say he was going to take her to an emergency clinic. Then he put her in the car and took her away. I lay by the door for several days, but Bernie didn't come back. A couple of nights later, Mom and Dad came home and sat down beside me. Dad massaged my ears and Mom hugged me until I could feel the heaving of her chest as she wept softly into the nape of my neck. That's when I knew Bernie wasn't coming back. I finally decided she must have gone someplace really special because who would want to a leave a great family and home like this? I missed her, but I was happy for her. I just wish I'd had a chance to **say goodbye.**

Maxim #14:

Never miss a **chance**
to tell those **closest** to you
that you **love** them.

But now, I was beginning to feel my age. I couldn't stand as straight and I couldn't make it out the doggie door before I started to poop. I had developed **disk disease,** which had killed the nerves in my hindquarters. I could no longer control simple bodily functions and I had trouble standing. Was it too much jumping up in the air? Well, probably not, but it didn't help either. I have no regrets though. It was so much fun!!!

After seeing Dr. Wight, Mom and Dad took me to see another specialist about back surgery. They decided not to put me through it. Instead, my parents adapted human adult diapers to prevent any accidents. It was a little inconvenient and I was a little embarrassed, but I adjusted because Mom and Dad were always there to help me maintain my dignity. My Dad started going with me to my groomer and he would hold me while she bathed and trimmed me. Airedales are very strong and can endure a lot of pain. Did my parents make the right decision? Could I have survived with a better quality of life? I think they made the best choice.

Maxim #15:

Aging is a **challenge,**
but adjusting to **change**
is easier with
a great **attitude**.

In the meantime, my parents thought a puppy might help revive me a bit and that's when that annoying, **devilish excuse** for a puppy named **Amber** came to live with us. Oh how that kid bugged me! I know she just wanted to play, but did I really ever aggravate Bernie that much?

Well, come to think of it, there was one time Bernie and I got really mad at each other. I was pretty young at the time and wanted Bernie to play, but she didn't want to. I kept teasing and pestering her until suddenly she lashed out. Before we really knew what was happening, Bernie bit my foot and I opened a gash above her eye.

My mom was trying to separate us and we bit her in the process and threw her to the ground. Mom was screaming and crying, and suddenly we realized what we had done and we stopped. Mom separated us and we both made a trip to see Dr. Wight to get fixed up. Later we learned that Bernie had Valley Fever and that was probably why she was so cranky at the time. So I guess in a way Amber and I were like that together, though I never really bit her. **I just wanted to.**

Although I had quit running with Dad and his friends long ago, Mom and Dad still took me places. One of my favorite places was our house in the mountains. I would lie in the shade of the Ponderosa pines and sniff the air, watch the birds and feel the cool grass beneath me. It was so peaceful most of the time, except for one of the first weekends after we moved there for the summer.

My mom and dad had gone out and I was home with Andrew and Grandma. While they were busy, I went out in the backyard.

"Look! The gate's open!"

I walked around the edge of the fence and into a neighbor's yard. The next thing I knew, I was being picked up by Animal Control and was hauled off to the local Humane Society. It was like **déjà vu** all over again!

Luckily, I wasn't there long before Dad, Mom and Andrew arrived to rescue me again! I was sitting in a kennel when I saw them running down the aisle toward me and I started a long, mournful cry. Dad threw open the kennel door and scooped me up in his arms. When he put me in the back of the van, I was so freaked out, I crawled all the way to the front just to be close to everyone.

HEELLPP!!!

This summer, life was getting to be more of a struggle. My back legs grew even weaker. When my family went away on vacation, it seemed like an eternity. But my dear sweet dog sitter came and stayed with me. Still, I really missed my family so I didn't eat for several days. My sitter didn't give up on me. Instead she cooked special things for me and hand fed me until I started feeling better. After that, I always tried to get up to see her when she came home. But the truth of the matter was I couldn't get up on my own any more. After my family came home, we were all so happy to see each other that I felt better. So we took one last trip to the mountains.

When we came home to the city summer heat though…oooh, it was so hot… it took my breath away. I didn't feel like eating and some days I just didn't want to get up. I saw my parent's worried faces, but I was always so happy to see them that I would somehow find the strength to get up, nudge their knees and rub their legs until they petted me.

Maxim #18:

When **times get tough,**
the smallest kindness
can **bring you joy**

Today, I lay on my bed and my mom and dad sat next to me, petting me and softly crying. I was feeling calm, surrounded by so much love. Suddenly from the other room, Amber barked. My dad left and when he came back, I looked up and saw my vet and her assistant. "Dr. Wight's here, Dr. Wight's here! Kelly, Kelly, Kelly!" I tried to get up, but Dr. Wight said, "Oh Max, don't get up, Max." She rubbed my head and my belly, "Goodbye Max! We love you, Max." She looked at my parents. "Are you ready?" she asked. Then I knew. They were here to help me—just like they always had. Yes, I'm ready.

What was that pinchin' my bottom? Oh, it just stung for a moment. No big deal. Aaaah, I feel so much love around me. It feels so nice, so warm. But I'm starting to feel so sleepy and it's funny—the pain is starting to go away. But I still feel my parents petting me, holding me. I know they love me. I hope they know how much I love them too. Mmmm…oh my, that's a bright light! Who's that? Bernie, is that you? Ouch! Quit biting my head! What do you mean, where have I been? Where have you been?! Look Bernie, I can run. I can jump. Wow! Ah Bernie, I love it when you lick my ears. Aaaaah-mmmmm! Ohhhh, Bernie! This is gonna be a great day!

And so it is…

Bernie, quit biting my head!

Epilogue

Life is full of lessons and it isn't always easy or what you expect. Still, that's no reason to put your tail between your legs and hide. It's good for the soul to leap in the air, wag your tail and howl at the moon from time to time. With all its challenges and disappointment, you can still have a great life! Resolve to be happy, courageous and grateful for every teacher who leads you—even if it's **the one on the end of the leash.**

Maxim #20:

Live Life to the Max!

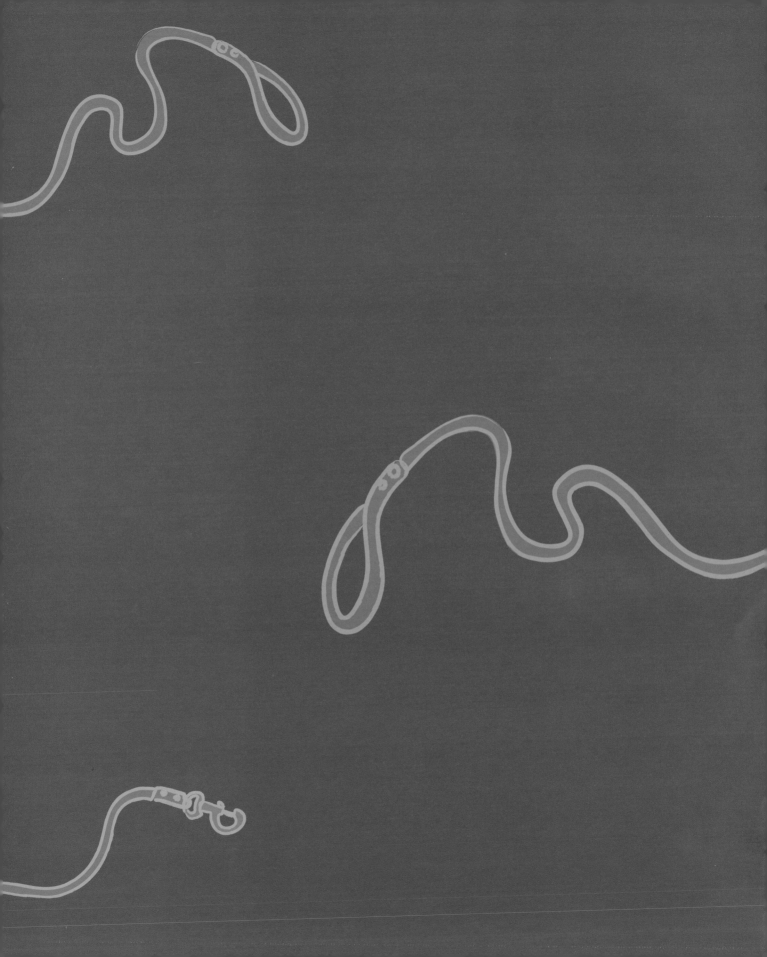

Send Us Your Own Max Stories

According to lists accumulated by the country's leading pet identification tag makers and pet insurance providers, the number one most popular name for a male dog is Max. If you have learned a special lesson from the Max in your life—no matter what breed—we would like to include his story in our sequel: *Life to the Max: More Maxims for a Great Life.* Please send your stories and photos to max@nicecreative.com. Photos should be scanned at 300 pixels-per-inch and should not include any copyrighted material. (Please contact us for transfer instructions if your files are more than 10MB.) You may also mail your material to: NICE Creative, 4645 South Lakeshore Drive, Suite 16, Tempe, AZ 85281. However, photos and other submitted material will not be returned.

Give the Gift of "Life to the Max"

To share this book with other dog lovers, you may purchase copies at www.lifetomax.com.

53

Writer's Acknowledgements

My deepest appreciation to my design partner, Terry M. Rohrs, whose extraordinary talent coupled with her enduring patience enabled me to finally bring this story to life; to Rene M. Rohrs (the Comma Queen) for her excellent proofreading and incisive feedback; to Dr. Tracy Wight, Dr. Karen Claus and the staff at McClintock Animal Care Center for caring and supporting us like family; to Shelly Ambrose at Shelly's Pet Grooming for always accommodating us in every way; to friends and family—like Mary Jones, Karen, Jose, Conrad, and Madison Laboy, Laurel Whisler, Bob and Carol Massingil, Don Dillon, Tessie McCabe, Peggy Morley, Linda Macklem, and my mom, Lois C. Reynolds, who encouraged me to publish this book; to Vince Schwartz and Jeff Noble (the Doodler and Giggler) for their unwavering friendship and insight; to Gayle Shanks of Changing Hands Bookstore and fellow author, Mary Marcdante, who provided invaluable feedback and support; to my husband, Lenny, for sharing this journey with me with love, inspiration and humor; and to Bernie, Max and Amber who have made our lives richer with their presence.